A Red Fox Book

Published by Random House Children's Books
20 Vauxhall Bridge Road, London SW1V 2SA

A division of Random House UK Ltd
London Melbourne Sydney Auckland
Johannesburg and agencies throughout the world

1 3 5 7 9 10 8 6 4 2

First published in Great Britain by Julia MacRae 1993

Red Fox edition 1999

Printed in Singapore

RANDOM HOUSE UK Limited Reg. No. 954009

ISBN 0 091 87293 6

FRASER'S
grump

SUE HEAP

RED FOX

For Mary and Geoff
and Nicholas

Fraser was in a grump.

So he headed off to his favourite tree ...

wearing his dad's kagoul and his sister's knapsack.

And just as he sat down
Buster the dog came up wagging his tail.

"Oh no!" sighed Fraser.
"Buster, you'd better be
quiet if you want to stay
under the tree with me."

But Buster didn't want to
stay under a tree keeping
quiet. Buster wanted to bark.
So he went and barked at the cat.

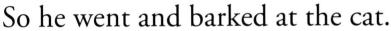

The cat hissed ...

... and went to join Fraser under the tree.

Buster barked at the tortoise.

The tortoise got up slowly ...

... and went to join Fraser
and the cat under the tree.

Buster barked at the hen.

The hen stopped pecking ...

... and went to join Fraser and
the cat and the tortoise under the tree.

Buster barked at the rabbit.

The rabbit leapt into the air ...

... and went to join Fraser and the cat
and the tortoise and the hen under the tree.

Buster barked
at the heron.

The heron hastily
folded his newspaper ...

... and went to join Fraser and the cat and the tortoise

and the hen and the rabbit under the tree.

Up came Buster.
"Sssssh!" said Fraser.

But Buster wasn't barking.
He was carrying a letter.
The letter said:

Please come home
Fraser. Lunch is
ready. love Mum x
P.S. Dad needs his Kagoul!
P.P.S. Jane says you can
keep her Knapsack
till Friday x.

Fraser yelled, "WOOF!" Buster wagged his tail. Fraser put the letter in his pocket.

"SSSSSSHH!" said the cat and the tortoise and the hen and the rabbit and the heron under the tree.

So Fraser and Buster very
quietly went away from the tree.

Then very noisily raced each other home for lunch.